A
WARRIOR'S SHATTERED
FATE

Written by

Maggie Frazer

Published in the United States of America by:

Cobb Publishing
704 E. Main St.
Charleston, AR 72933
https://CobbPublishing.com
Editor@CobbPublishing.com

ISBN-13: 978-1-960858-48-1

Dedicated to:

Mom, Dad, Evan, Ryan, Gracie, Gigi, Bebop, Christian (the best editor the planet has ever seen!) & Samuel, my amazing family.

(and my superb dog)

You all give me excellent ideas.

CONTENTS

Chapter One

I look up from my perch where me and my sister were smooshed together in one chair; the only chair we own.

"Sapphire, could you go and get dinner please?" my sister looks up from her book to ask the question.

"Yes Ruelian, I know the drill." I answer.

She smiles and goes back to her book. I walk out the door and grab my bow and arrow on the way.

The wooden door shuts as a result of my force, and I stumble into the snowy forest.

The owls are unusually silent. I believe it's because it is day-time, that's why. I'm just used to hunting at night. That's all.

The snow continues to fall on my flushed cheeks, and I perch on the rock located outside the hollow where wolves and other creatures of the sort make their nests.

I looked at the glowing mushrooms, and thought of how peculiar it was that they only glowed at night.

I'm used to hunting at night, and it's day. The forest can completely transform depending on what type of day it is.

I observe as I look around.

* * * * *

The mushrooms glowed a mischievous blue and sometimes switched, but only if you blinked. The olden times fancied that they

1

had a secret message to the Amphelem beings, a mysterious tribe that had the power to reveal all magic within the magical forest of Taeviios.

The Amphelem were reported to have pure white hair and tan skin, and with eyes that revealed no secrets.

I perch on the smooth stone and await a deer, or perhaps a wolf, or a leopard?

The sun burnt down on my not-so-fair skin.

And there! There was an antelope emerging from the den where it made its bed. I whip out my arrows, quiet as Blazeworm, and loosed an arrow at the prey.

It leaped, escaping the prison of death, and I cursed under my breath, with a shot of guilt. It had been stupid of me to think that I would get a leopard, when I couldn't even get an antelope.

There is a ripple in the Frostberry bush, and I look up, wondering if it was a thrush, another creature of the sort.

But when I looked up, there was a scared Amphelem, running away from my presence.

I could tell from the way he was moving that he was scared, so naturally I chased after him, curiosity winning control of my body.

He was running at quite a speed, and I found it difficult to keep up.

"Stop!" He yelps, as I do the opposite. *Sapphire you should care more for others, you should listen to them, you should value their opinion.* My sister's voice runs through my thoughts, and I slow to a pace.

"Why aren't you listening to me!" he yelled, trying to get me to stop. I stopped, but he didn't, he went on about a mile ahead, I estimate. But it is not exact because of the trees blocking my view.

Once he is far enough away I start to follow him, quietly, but quickly. A couple of hours later, I arrive at a village entrance, it was private and surrounded by a gate.

I hear voices coming from the inside, and as usual curiosity overtakes me.

I rest at the top of the tall, wooden gate and listen. The terrified Amphelem reports:

"A mortal here to kill, I watched her try to take the life of a female Theolo, it was a flame of an experience to watch one of our so-called allies try to take the life of a harmless creature that brings life to the world,"

I listen to him, sadness and anger filling my heart and soul. Why was he calling it a Theolo? Do they have different names for animals? Or was his language slurred?

"Yes that is a pity," I watch the seemed-to-be leader respond. "Rumor has it that the mortals use Theolo, and other animals as food. They have nothing else, don't hold it against her, Ronin, she was probably just feeding her family."

I dart away, holding back tears. And then spend the next hour running home.

I enter the stable to tend to Reo and Indigo, my two dragons.

They are happily cuddling, and I smile when they run to me.

Indigo, the smallest, leaped into the air to fly to me, and fell, not yet being able to fly.

The larger gold one, Reo scoffed at her dragonet, "Indigo, I'll be surprised if your wings aren't permanently scarred by the time you can fly."

"Well this is the only way to learn to fly; By jumping up in the air, and epically crashing to the unforgiving floor!" Indigo beamed.

I watched my little blue and violet dragon wave her wings in exasperation with her mother.

"Well yes, that is a very tremendous, heroic, and chaotic way to do it." Reo announced snarkily, as she smiles down at her daughter.

"Come on Indigo, time to scratch off your access scales." I called.

Indigo scrambled to my feet, excited. This was her favorite part of the day.

"Reo, I suppose you can handle yourself?" She nods and begins scratching her gold and black scales against the wooden wall. I nod and go tend to Indigo.

When I walk back into the small wood cabin I spot Ruelian in the corner, knitting her current project.

"I see you have come home empty handed." Ruelian glared at me—and I glared back.

"I had a long and unsuccessful hunt, could you leave me alone for once?" I grumped at her, stomping down the back hall to our room.

4

The fact that we had to sleep in the same room was altogether too much.

"You know this means that we won't have dinner tonight!" my sister yells from the other room, I ignore her and fall into a painful sleep.

Chapter Two

I blow dust off the book in my hand, the stench of earthy mushrooms and underbrush filling my strong but sensitive nostrils.

Suddenly a great amount of dirt falls from the ceiling, a couple of feet away, signaling that there is someone on the outside walking over my underground tunnel (which is to be expected).

I leap out of my small opening, shielding myself from dirt collapsing in on me.

In front of me was a fierce-looking girl, about my age (14). She possessed a weapon—a bow and arrow—and she looked ready to use it.

"Fancy seeing you out here!" I greeted.

"Not really."

I look at her, she looks at me, "I see you are not having the best of days," I survey.

She kneels down and says, "Well honestly, would you be having the best of days if you hadn't yet had breakfast, or dinner the night before?"

She frowned.

I decided to do the thing I always do; cause mischief! "Well, I wouldn't know because I always eat mushrooms, or basil leaves for my meal times."

The stranger grunted. "I guess I should introduce myself before you take up the whole day talking about yourself. Because I already know that you're the type of person who would do that. I'm Sapphire."

I look at the girl, Sapphire, *she is a grumpy fellow* I think to myself.

She looks at me expectantly.

"Ah yes, I'm Autumn," My snowy white owl flies down from her perch, and digs her claws into my shoulder, frightening Sapphire. "This is Meredith," I introduce.

She slowly stands up and holds a hand out. I smile as she does so. Meredith holds out her wings but nozzles Sapphire.

"I have a pet too!" the smile on her face she has rid herself of. "Two dragons, a mother and daughter."

"Wow! I always wanted a dragon, perhaps a Woodlan one." I told her.

"I have a Bronze one, and her daughter is a River dragonet, I think the father was a River dragon as well."

We talked for a while longer and as the day went by, I gradually realized so, and soon enough Sapphire realized it was time for her to depart.

"I have to get a meal for me and my sister."

She leaves, and somehow I feel she will be back.

* * * * *

The next morning I woke, and as usual I drank my morning tea and tended to my gardens above my underground hollow, and the ones below. After this I went to go see what Reed was up to. One of my best friends.

I knocked on the door that I helped him build, when we built his house. He opened the door with a smile.

"Hello!" I greeted.

"Hey!" he answered. "Come in and we can have some herbal tea, and lavender macaroons."

I gladly stepped into the wooden interior I was so familiar with.

He led me to the tiny eating area. "So what's new with you, Autumn?" he asked with a present grin.

"Well, yesterday I was having my lunch, and a very intense girl, about my age came walking over to my house."

He giggled.

"What?!" I proclaim.

"Sorry, it's just you literally live underground," he was unable to wipe the laugh off his face.

"Well anyway, she walks over to my house and of course, being the person that I am, I come out of my mushroom-filled home, and then she stands in front of me, looking fierce as ever, and then we just automatically become friends, it was awesome!"

"Oh, like that doesn't happen every time you meet someone." Reed commented.

I sip my tea pleasantly.

"Remember the time when you were telling me about your dreams of having a River dragon, and you accidentally dropped my godmother's favorite tea set that I was destined to use for the rest of my life," he paused dramatically, and then continued, "against my will. I was NOT going to be able to keep those clean, those things collected cobwebs like nobody's business!" his eyes sparked happily at the thought.

After the lovely spot of tea with Reed, I walked the long way home, enjoying the chill winds, clear skies, and red and orange highlights on the trees, which represented my name. After a long walk home that featured me considering the awe of the hawks that ruled the sky, and me admiring the squirrels' agility and talent to taunt the coyotes, but never wavering the foxes, I took up the responsibility of cleaning and caring for the hollow of which I made my home.

I mended the hole in my wall, cleaned the few dishes that happened to make their way into the small wooden sink, and then I worked on the washing. I patched up an annoying rip in my flowered olive and beige sweater. Then I watered all my many plants, except for the ones that did not need it. And then I finally had some time to do what I wanted. So I decided to work on a new sketch. And then I carefully made dinner. And then collapsed onto my bed.

Chapter Three

I wake up to the clanking and bumping of my sister banging around in the kitchen. At first it is hard for me to get out of the small cot I lay in.

"You're up." Ruelian commented.

"And what's the problem with that?" I snap.

"Nothing! absolutely nothing." She rolls her eyes.

I decided to leave the conversation where it was.

After breakfast I go out on a long hunt, to hopefully catch something, but probably just end up thinking and walking through the endless nothingness.

After I had walked most of the forest, I stumbled across a patch of Blueflame tulips, and stopped to see if I would get a glow. This was a very important plant. If you got a certain color of glow, it would determine your future, and how positive it was. Electric blue for a bright and positive future, a deep and shameful purple for a screwed and horrid future.

The tulips glowed purple. Clear as day. And terrible as death.

I stumble backwards and lose air for a few terrible seconds. The first thing I think of is if Autumn would help me fix my life.

Probably not, she barely knows me. I scolded myself.

But still, I find myself trekking through the forest trying to locate her underground home. I soon find her home and she walks out, dazed and confused.

"What the heck!" she yells, but smiles to herself. "I knew you would come back!" she exclaimed. "What are you doing here? Oh, say no more. Let's go inside and get some tea."

I roll my eyes, despite my desperate state. "Well you didn't even give me a chance to even speak," I quietly mutter to myself. But walk in.

"So, Autumn, you know the magic tulips that tell you your positive or unpositive fate? Well I have come upon one, and need you to help me," I paused to let her catch up to my hasty words.

"Wow," She looked astonished, I would be too (and I was). "Well, the first thing we should do is to go to the keeper of fate,"

"What's the keeper of fate!?" I loudly interrupted.

"The keeper of fate is a fairy that can see anything about you and know anything about you. If you let her, she can look back in your past, and tell you where you screwed up." Autumn took a breath for air,

"Sounds useful," I commented. "Will you go with me? To ask?" I held my breath waiting for an answer.

"I have nothing better to do," was Autumn's solitary answer.

I let out my breath, yes Autumn was practically a stranger, but it was still comforting to know that I wouldn't be alone on the journey.

Autumn's style of packing was quite unordinary, she packed ONE OUTFIT, then packed TWENTY books, then she packed literally all of the little beanies that she knits (which you had to admit where very well done, intricately woven with white and yellow flowered, stunning butterflies neatly adorned with electric blue stripes, covering most of the black layer under the stripes).

"What. Is. That?" I asked, judging her suitcase, which wasn't even a suitcase, it was a knitted bag with a floral pattern.

"This," she smiled, "is my bag that I made when I was… I don't actually know how old, but younger."

I shook my head, and then decided to tell her that I was going to pack my things—the things I actually NEEDED.

When I entered my home, my sister was cooking dinner for two, it made me surge with guilt as I realized that I would have to tell her about all that had happened.

"That's you isn't it, Sapphire?"

I cringed, wanting so bad to tell her I was a stranger, but Ruelian didn't fall for things like that, and I knew it wouldn't work this time.

"Yes it's me, Ruelian." I answered.

"Supper is almost ready," she called.

I hurriedly ran upstairs, packed a few outfits, a notebook, and a sack to sleep in, but I soon grabbed another because I knew that Autumn wouldn't remember hers.

After this it was time for supper with my sister. I knew what I had to do, and I was dreading it.

"So, any food you caught today?" Ruelian asked conversationally.

My stomach sank. "Well, actually no."

Her face sank.

"BUT," I quickly added, "I did get some fresh air." I hoped that would keep her face from falling even lower.

I put down my fork. "Ruelian, there's something I need to tell you."

She took a nervous swallow, and listened.

"So you know those magic tulips that tell you your fate?" I rushed. "Well I've found one, and let's just say that I need to investigate some. Is that ok?"

She was quiet for a moment, and then: "Well, you are fourteen, I trust that you will be responsible and careful."

I let out the breath that I was very aware I was holding.

"Thank you," was all I could manage.

Then I finish my dinner, say my goodbyes, and set out.

* * * * *

Autumn was waiting by a birch tree, her freakishly white owl napping in an upright position on Autumn's shoulder.

"Hello," I briskly greeted. We walked a few miles in silence, and then out of curiosity I decided to break the unusual silence between us.

"Do you have any family?" I casually asked.

"No. The first memories I have are of the Amphelem raising me and my older sister Hazel. They said I could live on my own in the forest once I turned thirteen, the age of maturity, they believed. My sister decided to stay with them, I miss her." Autumn quietly answers.

13

"I'm sorry." I conveyed my feelings.

"It's fine," she answers. But I knew it wasn't.

More silence for each mile.

Finally she asks; "Do you have any hobbies? I love knitting as you can see!"

I nod. "Um… I guess I find hunting enjoyable, the sitting around part is my favorite." I laugh.

She nodded and continued to make progress on the track.

About an hour later, the air started to smell quite funny, and the temperature got unusually warm. "Do you feel that?" I asked Autumn,

"Yeah, it does feel quite warm, and by the looks of it, I don't think the air is interested in the idea of cooling down,"

I nodded agreeably.

Instantly after she finished her sentence, the ground devolved into a sort of pixelated form, and a ball of wind caught me and Autumn as well as our stuff. Meredith was screeching in my ear while frantically trying to get away from her newfound enemy, this ball of wind.

"Sapphire grab my hand, trust me," Autumn's worried eyes pleaded.

At first I didn't want to listen to her, but then I realized the fate of the situation, and grabbed her elegant fingers.

Then, all was quiet.

Chapter Four

I was laying on the hard cement, Autumn was next to me. It was clear that we had been unconscious and were just waking up. Huge dark blue, green, and yellow buildings loomed over us, creating a menacing effect. I shook Autumn, still in her trance.

"What, GRAB THE MUSHROOMS!" She yelled, just waking up.

"Don't worry about mushrooms, we have bigger problems!" I snap.

She blinked, clearly not understanding me.

"I think we were teleported to another dimension," I hurriedly told her.

"Oh."

I roll my eyes, and pick her up, waiting for her teleportation effects to wear off.

I began to realize that we must be somewhere in Europe, given the bright color scheme. It seemed to be the early 1800's. Everyone was dressed in dreamy hats and dresses. The women wore lipstick and had beautiful hairstyles, and the men were wearing suits, gently holding the delicate hands of the females.

"This looks like it is a little earlier than our time," I whisper to Autumn.

"Yeah." She agrees, coming out of her trance.

We decided to walk around for a bit, exploring the area, looking at the people on the side of the street, painting, playing the saxophone, or juggling.

Once, there was a young woman carrying two pythons, and another wound around her neck. She had offered us to come to her pet tent, but when Meredith hissed at her she skidded away, embarrassed to be afraid.

After that we moved on, Not stopping at the tempting food shops, or falling for the jeweler's flattering comments.

But we soon learned from gossip on the street that the main business hall was a giant building that was intricately painted midnight blue, located in the center of the city they were stationed at.

"What are we going to do?" Autumn asked.

"The only thing that I can think of to do right now, is to wander the streets until this thing-a-ma-bob decides to teleport us to somewhere else," I answer.

"Well, we could do that, or we could wait for a fortune teller, or a past reader, maybe a magician of some sort. Eh?"

I consider her idea, "But then again, we don't know how to find a magician."

"Well they're not the sort of beings that you look for, they come to you," Autumn annoyingly corrected.

Suddenly cold hands wrapped around my mouth, *A STALKER!* I wrath, and kick, but the next thing I knew, I was being thrown into a black carriage, and Autumn was not.

* * * * *

16

Tragically terrible singing was being screeched in my ear. It was a female voice. I clutch my head. The first thing I remember is getting shoved into this black carriage, and Autumn looking desperately at me.

The singing intensified. I crawled slowly to the moving carriage's window, and looked up, what I could see; striped socks that smelled of age, and fine black Victorian dresses. *Witches,* I concluded, I kicked the metal railing trying to get the attention of the singing witches.

"Quiet down there!" They hollered. I scowled, and rolled over.

What I could tell about the atmosphere was that we were in the middle of nowhere, and that it was desperately chilly. I didn't know where I was or if I had been teleported, but I did know that I really hated those witches.

We rode for hours, suddenly the carriage was pulling into a courtyard, with a ton of other sketchy looking witches, and I did not like it.

I was uncomfortable.

When the witches pulled the cart to a complete stop, I found them opening the hatch they had used to transport me into this terrible concoction.

"Get the chains ladies!" one of the cruel witches ordered.

They tossed the pair of chains to each other, and the next thing I knew, I was being strapped onto hard metal, in other words, known as the dreadful idea of chains.

Then they harshly guided me through the looming mansion, which seemed to be a big house for all of them; on the inside, shady rap-disco music played, and there were fog machines everywhere, exhaling a spooky and delightfully dreadful atmosphere.

The witches seemed to be constantly consuming some sort of drink, whether it was a red wine, or a clear vodka. Either way the whole place was stupendously awful, and I hated it.

There also seemed to be lighting that worked with the black-painted-walls. It appeared to be commonly recognized as a red-or-ange, or a toxic green.

The witches themselves seemed to wear all black, and had almost pure white skin, and usually had some sort of braid or up-do for their varied colored hair. But I noted that they never wore hats, like the witches in fairy tales, because these witches were too evil to be even slightly similar to the bad guys you read about in stories.

I was dragged into a big room, slightly similar to the previous rooms, but this one was much larger than the others, and had cages hanging from the ceiling, gold-rimmed, round cages, containing beautiful mystical birds that were far more gorgeous than any bird you would expect to find in a modern country such as Europe.

But at the front of the room was a woman with pure white skin, hair as red as blood, and eyes a startling blue like the aqua marine blue ocean.

"Queen Voracious."

The witch that was leading the way called out to her. The Queen was sitting on a throne in a rather disturbing position. She was drinking out of clear glass, inside it was what seemed to be a viciously dark green drink that looked like if it spilled, the steam coming from it would suffocate you.

"Yes," she answered, in a queenly, but dangerously sly voice.

"We have another prisoner."

The queen set her intense gaze on me. "Bring her here," she groaned in a bored but still queenly voice.

"Why am I here?" I shouted at her, having no fear of her serpentine eyes, or her serene authority.

"So," the queen announced.

I rolled my eyes.

"You are here because I simply want you to be, and because you have come here from another dimension. I can sense it on you, and I want to know how you did that."

I couldn't believe her. Yes I knew she seemed to be the main authority, But seriously was giving full-on Mary Poppins vibes.

"Well, what are you going to do to me?" I asked, shooting back her bored voice.

"Well I guess we could put you in the dungeon until I remember you exist."

Now her bored voice catching on a more depressed tone, but fooling no one.

With that the witches grabbed hold of my freezing cold skin, and yet again dragged me through halls, staircases, and an occasional balcony, letting me glimpse a view of beautiful Europe.

* * * * *

It was dark in the prison cell they had led me to. It was also very damp, pretty much the same as all prison cells, I decided to eat the classic stale French bread they had given me, best eat things as soon as they're given to you, because then you could get them as best they were.

I decided to settle into the musty cold cell, and survey the prisoners.

There was a man who looked about the age of sixty, and had a classical long white beard that you would not be surprised about (or interested in).

In the cell straight across from me was a hissing old lady. She looked as if she hadn't had food in over a month, which I strongly believed was so.

And then a few cells over, was a small girl with an olive hood over her. She seemed to be shaking from either tears or being too cold for too long. Her short dress-tunic was of the sack material, and was the color of grass shifting from fresh summer grass to tan autumn grass.

I threw a cloth laying on my bed toward her gently, coming from a place of sympathy, not harm.

She looked up, face drenched in sweat and tears, I quickly wrote on a fresh piece of paper from my pocket notebook; it read:

Are you ok? (*Probably not*, I thought as I wrote.)

Do you know anything about this place,

Do you have parents, or a guardian?

Then on at the end of the small slice of paper I wrote;

(answer on the back of the paper.)

Then I slid it over to her.

I watched her write, and then she slid the paper back to me. On the back it read;

No I'm not ok,

I was orphaned when the queen took me from my parents and killed them.

My name is Olive and no I don't know much about this place except that it is absolutely dreadful. And that it is full of stuck-up witches,

I am also ten years old.

I looked at her, then put on a friendly smile. She gave a sad but hopeful smile back.

She struck me as a very honest little girl, but very good at reading people and figuring out who to trust. Looking at her dark skin and windblown black hair made think of how this girl had once had a family and now she didn't. I remembered how I had chosen to leave mine, to figure out my fate.

But this girl seemed to be also good at putting on a big act, to fool anyone she needed to. I collected that she would be very useful. But then I furiously scolded myself for having such a heartless Idea.

Olive soon went to sleep, and I decided to contemplate every possible way to get out of this cell, and soon I found myself getting extremely tired—but I refused to give into sleep just yet.

I wonder about Olive, was she depressed (probably), did she have any pets (this was a stupid question), but nevertheless here I was having it, and if I can tell you one thing besides the fact that Autumn was annoying, it's that I'm not stupid.

My train of thoughts kept spinning for another long, dreadful hour in this dreary place. It was seriously the last place on earth you would want to be, especially if you are stuck in it—for probably the next few years until some dreadfully boring queen decides to do something with you.

Then, alas, I desperately and terribly drifted into a restless sleep, but I mean there wasn't really another, or better, thing to do when you are under the watchful eye of dangerous witches.

They truly were terrible and I didn't want to do anything that they might call me out for, the opposite attitude that I had when I was in the presence of the shallow queen.

And then finally, I was asleep.

Chapter Five

I had been wandering the streets of Europe, enjoying the sweet aroma of coffee, and quiches.

I had happily chatted with a friendly old man, who was playing an accordion. We talked about his music history, and I had told him about Meredith my owl, which he had politely inquired about.

It had been about two hours since then, so about two and a half hours since me and Sapphire were separated. But I wasn't worried about her, I knew she could handle herself out there, she was fiercer than the Greek god Mars, or whatever his name was.

Meredith and I continued to float between the cities, it was all really quite peaceful, and I was beyond content. But I didn't know if I was going to be teleported at any given moment, and that was pretty much the only thing that was poking at my comfort.

* * * * *

"Honestly Autumn, I don't think I can allow you back in this shop. It is not in a custom to completely skip over paying, especially when you have already eaten our food, it is not the way of life." the storekeeper patiently, but annoyingly explained to me. "You're being contrary." he conveyed in a mild tone.

"Maybe, but you see I don't have fifteen, I only have twelve, and I really must go, sir. Can I please just pay and go, make things easier for both of us? Doesn't that sound fun?"

"Uh fine, but you are so annoying, I do not appreciate that."

"Dang," I slurred.

Then I happily trotted out of the store, feeling delighted with myself.

A few hours later I walk into another store, preparing myself for another argument. "Good morning!" I happily announce to the entire coffee shop. They glance at me as if I am a lunatic (I am). Then I prance over to the front of the coffee shop, to order a frappuccino.

The cash register looks at me with sad eyes, "What can I get you?" He narrated.

"Could I get a frappuccino? Please? How much are they? I only have ten." I asked with a bright smile on my face.

"We love to see you smile," He droned.

I decided that this guy was not having the best of days, and handed him a bit of my money.

His face brightened at the sight and then he got me the frappuccino, and I paid him the rest of my money.

The day was long and hard. I didn't know what to do. I couldn't spend any money, because I didn't have any. *What a shame.*

Meredith suddenly flew off into the big cloudy sky. Bored, I decided to follow her. She flew into one of the looming oaks. I didn't exactly know why she was or what she had spotted, but I could hear a bunch of wing beats coming from the enormous tree. I could also see—wait, purple wings? And they were scaly, like a crocodile, but of course it wasn't a crocodile because they didn't fly, and they weren't purple.

Then my mind jumped to the possible answer, a dragon. I whistled, trying to protect my owl from the rare and dangerous creature's fire, or rough play, but Meredith wouldn't listen.

After a few more whistles, a man walked up. a couple minutes later as he got closer, I realized that it was the same man in which I had bargained with, earlier at the first shop.

"Good day!" I greeted, even though drawing attention to myself was probably not the best idea. Meredith was still fighting with the dragon, and I was worried for her life, but if she wasn't going to listen to me, what else could I do? She was being stupid, so there.

"Listen, Kid," the storekeeper interjected, "I was wrong to bully you just because you didn't have enough money, mind you, you were also wrong to eat my food, knowing you didn't have enough, but I just wanted you to know that I truly apologize, and, didn't want any hard feelings."

"You seem like a kind fellow," I complimented, "I nearly forgot about all of this, I don't hate you, I was wrong, it was very wrong of me to eat when I knew I didn't have enough. I'm sorry."

He smiled, But just as his eyes were crinkling, as one's eyes do when smiling, the ball of familiar wind started to encircle me.

My thoughts reflected one word—*No!*

The wind was howling in my ear, and I had the strangest idea. Maybe time travel appeared every time you were interacting with someone, and were not all that comfortable in the situation.

I closed my eyes, worrying, waiting, and hoping. What if Sapphire and I never found each other again? What if she was stuck with the terrible witches that took her? My heart was hurting. I hated myself for not doing something, anything, when they took her.

And then, all was still.

* * * * *

This time I was in a very snowy setting, everything was quiet, and mystic, which is just about my least favorite type of vibe.

The snow had a natural blue tint in it.

But one of the most obvious things about the area was the beautifully white-dusted pine trees, colored the deepest, richest green that you could imagine, but still not a dusty, or muddy green. It was a green to be remembered, a green that no one could capture in a painting, a green of life. I took a breath in. I did have to admit that it was extremely pretty, even if it wasn't my cup of tea.

And another thing that was especially unique to the scenery, was the small rare purple flowers, tentatively peeking out of the places with frost. The flowers shied away from the heavy clumps of snow.

After taking in another glance at the terrain, I set off to explore, and maybe find some sort of person, because I would die without attention.

I observed a great deal of animals, mostly birds of various sorts. A snowy owl here, another there.

I shed a tear, remembering my own owl. *I hope she is ok, I hope she'll find a fine home out there*.

I soon came to yet another small village. Again, I roamed the lonely streets. Inside I could hear sounds of lively parties, and festive chants, even though it was nowhere near any holiday.

My eyes fell upon a gray outline of a man walking towards me. I started to get uneasy, but I held myself together. When he got closer, I realized that he was the same man from the first shop I had gone to in Europe. This was now our third encounter. What was it with this guy and his habit of following me?

It was getting disturbing. Annoyed, I lazily lifted my arm, put on a fake smile, and waved.

But wait! There was something draped on his shoulders that wasn't his apron. It was Meredith! I was so happy inside, I almost snatched her right off the old man's shoulder. He smiled as he viewed my impulse.

He lifted Meredith from his shoulder, and she flew out of his arms, and nozzled me, then took her seat on *my* shoulder.

"Thank you," I managed.

"How did you get here?" he asked.

I decided to tell the truth. "I came here from time travel, I think."

He nods. "I don't know how I got here, but I think I was brought with you maybe?"

A new theory starts to buzz in my head: does time travel only take the people that you're interacting with, or does it only work with two people? Questions played ping-pong in my mind, as I surveyed the forest, the kindly man in front of me.

Chapter Six

There was cold water falling on my face. I looked over at Olive, but when she made eye contact I found her face a wet mess. "I am going to get you out of here," I quietly whispered to her.

* * * * *

After a few hours, something interesting happened, for some reason. I didn't understand why. It was only a few days after I had been captured and taken to this prison, this next worst thing to hell.

The guard had come to ask If I had any money. Of course I had not answered, but she still plastered a screwy look on her face. I didn't much care about how she had been basically the rudest person in the world by asking that.

After a couple more rounds of staring at the ceiling, having depressed thoughts, and having the world's worst time, I had an idea.

I knocked over my bed so that it would make a huge loud crash, and as I had predicted, the guard who had asked me the outrageous question came running to see what had taken place.

"What the heck did you do? You're a big threat to my job, why do you have to make it worse?"

"I have a fabulous talent for causing trouble, all you're doing is encouraging me when you say things like that." I gave her a mischievous smile.

"What on earth do you mean?" she yelled in an exasperated voice.

I rolled my eyes in response. "Well, you can keep yelling at me about how I'm the worst threat this world has ever seen (I quite like it when you do, though). Or, you can get me out of here, and I will stop messing with you. And also, if you don't let me out, you will be breaking that little girl's heart over there," I pointed to Olive. "So you can keep bullying me, or you may kindly let me go, and I will spare your life."

Her face was as red as a tomato. "YOU KNOW WHAT, YOU ARE A COMPLETE PEST! AND I NEED A PUNISHMENT FOR YOU—NO, I HAVE A *PERFECT* PUNISHMENT FOR YOU."

She furiously stormed to one of the other halls, and came back into the cell room. She was carrying a pair of heavy chains that looked like they could hold twelve elephants, and not have any problem doing it.

"I'll show you how prisoners who don't listen get treated!" She roared at me.

All I did was blink at her.

She opened my cell door, but I didn't make a run for it. I knew better.

"These are the finest, strongest chains of the age, they have the strength of twelve elephants."

(I knew I was right about the elephants. I just *knew* it.)

"Well then, If they're so strong," I played, "why don't you prove it?"

"OH I'LL SHOW YOU, I'LL SHOW YOU IF IT TAKES ME TILL THE END OF TIME!"

And then, just as I had planned, she strapped the chains onto herself.

I happily strutted out through the open cell door, and smugly stole the keys that were hanging on a hook shaped like a disturbing witch hat, which was odd, because the witches didn't wear hats. All the while the self-imprisoned guard was yelling curses at me. I ignored her and went to unlock Olive.

The first thing she did when I unlocked her was run to me and hug my waist, for she only went half-way up my lengthy build.

"I'm so glad that I met you," she gasped through tears of happiness. I am not a fan of this emotional, huggy personality, but I guess for a small girl, it's fine.

I know if I take the keys with me, the prisoners might never get out, so I decided to leave them, but with that, we were off, to go find the world's most annoying being, AKA Autumn.

* * * * *

We had escaped the palace, but it was a hard process. It wasn't the first time I needed to weasel my way out of something.

The girl, Olive, silently walked next to me. She never said a word, unless I asked a question (I had previously asked just one).

We walked in boring, unargumentative silence for a while.

"So, do you have any other family that you left behind?" I hesitantly ask.

"Well, n-no." She answered.

I didn't believe her.

The silence followed me like pending doom, and the smell of smoke started to creep its way up my nostrils. A few snake python lengths away, there was... a glowing tree? *What?* It was glowing red-orange, making the white bark of the tree look like a luminescent beige, instead of an innocent white. I knew immediately that the tree was an evil sign.

Olive looked intrigued. she couldn't seem to pull her eyes away from it. Come to think of it, I couldn't either, and this infuriated me. I HATE stuff that can control me.

Suddenly my shoulders stung with the annoying pain of red liquid leaving your pale body. A screeching roar rung in my ear. All I could see was the willow tree, even though I knew that was not what was in front of me. How? Because I was on the ground, thrown to the ground by the wretched creature screaming bloody murder in my ear.

"I feel like I feel when I have Déjà vu," Olive whispered in a dreamy voice. I knew it was her drifting into a dais.

The screeching dulled as I heard a rustle of wings and the crunch of claws on chilled leaves.

I finally heard it all stop.

It had stopped so suddenly I almost wasn't ready. The creature was beginning to come into view. The first thing I noticed was the large amount of black and red-orange. The next was the long blue frill that was bestowed upon his head. The head was decorated with black stripes that looked like flames. His two wings were definitely the largest part of him, located above his hind legs, the only ones he owned. And lastly he had two eyes, that marked where two long antennae came out from his forehead.

"Sir!" Olive exclaimed. At first I had thought that she was just joking, but then she went on to introduce me to him. "This is Sir, he is the possessed guardian of the willow tree. He will help us. You know he is the shifter, permanently cursed as a wyvern. He used to be an Amphelem, extremely gifted, with the power to take the form of anything he wanted to, but then, a witch took him and turned him into a wyvern for a century. He is on his thirteenth year as a wyvern, but I know him from before I got captured. We used to go on rides together."

She took a breath from the stream of words she had just produced.

"Well?" I looked at Olive.

"The best thing I can say to do is to hop on him and see where he takes us. It's not like his curse can spread to us," She interjected logically.

I didn't know Olive very well, but there was one thing I did know, witches were popular, and we were sure to come across them some time.

We gratefully mounted Sir, and before we knew it, we were off!

The wind blew in our face, caused by Sir's black and red wings.

"He should be called plasma, or volcanic." Olive shared.

"Yes, he sure looks like it. I think Sir is VERY dignified though," I agreed.

* * * * *

When we landed it was dreary. We had flown over a few lakes and massive forests. It had been hard to not fall off. when I rode on any of my dragons I always wore a saddle.

Olive and I hopped down and examined the environment.

"What do you think we will find here?" I asked. I took a breath, and then I was surrounded by cherry blossoms. The world was suddenly busy, and there was a street not one hundred feet in front of us. And then I knew that we had time traveled. It was honestly getting annoying, and persistent by now, and why did it always have to be when I'M TALKING?

We walked into another environment (just when we were getting used to the old one).

A young woman with short curly red-ruby hair walked up to us. She was truly beautiful, with stunning blue eyes. She looked non-Japanese, more like she was from Canada, or a northern country, because she had pure white skin.

"Hey!" she said as she approached us, which seemed abnormal, coming from my introverted self. I pulled up my hood as a warning sign. She didn't seem to notice, but her face did change quickly, as if she was hearing something that hurt her feelings.

"Hi!" Olive greeted back. She didn't seem to notice that it was extremely unsafe to reply to people.

"I'm Kris, by the way, spelled with a K. Don't ask, because I'm going to tell you anyway. My mother was feeling possessive, and she didn't want to have me named after any-one, and since my father's name was Chris, spelled with a C, she went and was like 'I'M GOING TO PUT A K IN FRONT, NO ONE WILL EVER TOUCH HER, SHE IS ALL MINE.' Disturbing right? I mean, I probably would have done the same thing, but who cares, I might even change it one day, wouldn't that be cool? I could be called Jasmine, or Claudia, or AGATHA! Wouldn't it be cool to be called Agatha? I think so. Okay, I will shut up now because your face and thoughts are very disturbing—I MEAN FACE, NOT THOUGHTS."

I stared at her. I knew so much about her, and it hadn't even been five minutes.

She was for sure a beautiful person, and probably previously emotionally, or physically hurt in the past, because I knew that people do not naturally share that much about themselves as the literal second sentence they say to you.

She was definitely acting weird.

"Um—sorry if I sound weird," she interjected nervously. Kris tucked a strand of her gorgeous deep red hair behind one pierced ear. The ear had a small silver hoop on the top corner, the hoop had a black line going around it. It was absolutely stunning in my opinion, but Olive noticed and her face immediately crinkled.

"Well Kris, or Kristina? I am assuming that is your full name?"

"Yes," She answered.

"You seem like a very nice person. We are glad to be meeting you. Could we treat you to lunch? What type of food do you like?"

"Ah um, yes I would love that. I like sushi but I am honestly grateful for anything that I receive."

* * * * *

We walked for a while until we came across a cozy little shop that was selling coffee. Kristina settled for a nice latte, but I however chose something a little more dark as my soul, just a plain, black, iced coffee. No milk.

I wonder what Autumn was doing. It made me a little sad to think of her because I did miss her, as much as it hurt to admit. This was honestly a new low for me. I blinked to snap myself out of it. By now my coffee was almost half empty.

The shop was a pretty little shop. It had beautiful decorations of leaves and dragonflies woven into the leaves and some yarn flowers.

I wondered how long it had taken one person to do this, or maybe it had been a few. I didn't know.

"I—I noticed you had a dragon, or a wyvern? Well anyway I wanted to tell you that I went to school for dragon telepathy and I could give you some pointers, if you wanted them. My treat."

"Wow, that's so kind of you to offer, we would love that, but Sir won't let anyone touch him," I confirmed, periodically.

I put my hand on her shoulder. In most cultures, it is respectful to embrace a person, or to slowly touch them as a sign of peace or love. And that is what I was doing here.

Kristina was an interesting person and I wanted to get to know her, but she was also a separate person, that had feelings and a backstory, and I didn't know if she wanted me to know that or not. So I was simply going to leave her how she was. I know I have a bad habit of trying to change people. It is something I'm trying to work on. And hopefully I'm getting better, I don't know.

Me and Kris chatted for a while. We talked about our dragons, and how we had gotten here. She seemed so trustworthy, almost like magic. She was funny, and was extremely beautiful. She loved laughing and putting smiles on people's faces. She took away my frown. And I had to admit, I was having fun and I didn't want her to leave. Sometimes she was awkward, she would break off in sentences.

But it was worth it.

"So, used to be a rogue?" I asked, not sure I had heard, right. But at the same time being amazed. I was talking to a woman who had been a rogue, cast out of her tribe, her clan, her league, and had taken to the streets.

I thought it must be a sad, amazing life. But then angrily, I scolded myself. Of course it had been terrible for her. She had probably been sad. She had also probably missed her family, and I was mad at myself for thinking she might've enjoyed it.

"Yes, I am still, but I do have a few friends and I own a dragon. She's back at my cabin."

I was in awe. This woman not only had her own cabin, but she also had a dragon and a few friends, even skittish as she seemed. Maybe she did have an okay life.

"Take it back to my cabin, we could have tea. I mean I know we've already had coffee but still, I'm definitely a tea person over coffee, if you can't already tell. You could also meet my dragon. It would be fun."

"I don't know what to say," I answered.

"How about yes?" She cracked a beam, her blue eyes and deep red wavy hair matching perfectly with her pale skin, opening to reveal beautiful white teeth, forming a smile.

Kris, me and Olive walk through the woods to Sir. Olive serenely strokes his black, yellow, and magma red scales. He was a little scared at first because we had left him, but he soon got used to the change of situation.

Leaves crunch beneath my black boots as I hopped onto his back. It felt warm. I could tell he was building up a fire in case he needed it, a sign of stress.

Olive continued to stroke him, murmuring calm whispers to him. Kris was just there waiting for us to get Sir under control.

Once we got him to calm down, Kris mounted, and we were off flying through the brisk air. It was not exactly cold outside, but it was still absolutely not hot.

The wind streamed out my long hair. I hated tangles in it, but I wasn't exactly worried now because it was so thrilling and blissful to be out high above the Earth, soaring through the sky.

Light blue rivers floated beneath us, golden city lights shimmered below, and earthy green forests danced in gold, pink, and blue horizon.

This is what I loved, being in the sky riding on a regal creature.

* * * * *

A few minutes later, the sky started to darken. Was that a bad sign? (Probably…)

"Kris, is it always cloudy here?" I asked.

"Well, it does get cloudy often, so yes, maybe?"

Sir took a deep dive into the green forest, the smell of leaves and lush earth filled my nostrils. Once his claws hit the earthy ground, he walked for about five more miles, but it was rather fast, maybe even running, because he was such a big wyvern.

He finally stopped at a cabin. It had vines growing up its sides, and on the vines were pretty pink flowers, well cared for. Maybe Kris was a gardening person.

"Well, this looks like a cozy place," I complemented.

Olive nodded in agreement.

We hopped off of Sir, and Kris led the way to her wooden door. It opened with a squeal. I absolutely hate loud screeching sounds. I tried not to cringe.

She opened the door and revealed a cozy little home. There was a fire crackling, tea simmering, and a basket full of... cats!?

One tiny black one hopped over to me and began licking my hand that I hadn't realized was lowered to the kitten's reach. I kneeled down, cats being my spirit animal. I especially loved black ones.

The cat happily curled beside me, enjoying my warmth. She batted at my hands whenever I stopped scratching her.

"That's Jemima, named after Jemima Puddle-Duck, from the Peter Rabbit story," Kris added nervously. "I found her strutting through the forest pretending like she had a purpose in life."

"Sounds like me," I laughed.

"Well now she does," Kris winked

"What–uh-no, I cannot have another animal in my life. I already have two dragons, Kris."

"All the more reason. Cats and dragons get along well, especially babies."

I huffed. She was going to make sure that Jemima went home with me. I didn't bother resisting. I knew she wanted me to have her, and I did want the kitten. After all, it looks so helpless and meek at my feet.

The tea was steaming on the stove so Kris went to go get it. She got out three clear glass cups and poured warble tea into them. She surprisingly got out a small cat-feeding bowl, poured some more tea into there, and added a spot of milk. She then took it over to Jemima and Jemima happily started to lick it up!

I stared at Kris, awestruck. The cat was happy as could be, just drinking her tea like a true British cat.

"You're feeding your cats tea?" I asked when she didn't explain her behavior.

"Well why not?" she retorted.

"I mean, just asking," I quickly added after she had finished.

Olive silently watched the whole affair, with critical eyes.

"So what do you think of having an archery contest? Have you done archery in the past years?" Kris spontaneously asked.

"We would love that, I have, I don't know if Olive—"

"Oh, she can just judge the contest, I mean, have you Olive?"

"No," she quietly answered.

"Then you can be the judge for the contest, okay?" Kris explained.

It didn't sound like a question.

* * * * *

An arrow went flying through the air, shot by me. It flew a little further, then straight on target.

Kristina's mouth dropped. "I can barely get it on the target!" she yelled, shocked. "I did not know that you would be that talented, are you a hunter or something?"

I quickly nodded, hating the attention, but that is just part of life, being uncomfortable. I was sort of getting used to it, with the jumping between different worlds and all.

We practiced till the sun went down, and Kris took us back to her cozy home, gave us another spot of tea, and then as much as I hate to admit it, we teleported, again.

* * * * *

The world was quiet this time, not as overwhelming as the last times, because we were so used to it. Well, maybe not Olive, but she did have rather a talent for staying calm, collected, and quiet for the shebang of things that were happening in her life.

The world started to come into view, and I saw yet another forest coming to the light. It looked and felt like my home forest. It probably was. I had read somewhere, or maybe Autumn had told me, that you can feel if you are in the forest of your birth, somewhere deep in you DNA there is a gene that recognizes the place you are born, the place where you made your first memories.

That was pretty much all the info I had about it.

"Olive, this is my home forest," I told her without actually meaning to.

"Wow, really, how do you know?" This was Kris.

"It's written in my blood, you would know too, if you thought about it," I answered her.

"Hmm," Kris added thoughtfully.

And with that they went for a long walk through the woods, all animals intact. Even Jemima.

Chapter Seven

And then of course, Just like that, I was back in the forest, the earthy ground beneath, the forest where I had built my underground home, the forest where I had been left by my family, because I had not met the expectations for their beauty standards. It was tragic for me to think about of course, but I would not have wanted to live with them if they were going to scowl every time they looked at me. What life would that be?

My owl Meredith was now somehow on my shoulder. Thank God, I was about to lose it if she got lost.

I spotted a mouse and pointed it out for her so that she didn't dig her sharp claws into my poor dark skin when she was hungry.

She quickly caught it between her claws and ate it.

I watch her rip apart the mouse; everything has a cycle. If owls didn't eat mice, then the world would be overpopulated with mice. If mice did not eat insects, then that would be a gigantic problem, coming from me, Autumn, AKA insects' worst enemy.

I wandered my home woods alone with Meredith. We had a long time to wait before something happened, so I opened my pocket full of pastries that I had snuck (hah), and began to eat.

I worked on coming up with ways to work on knitting, reviewing all the ways that you could make knots and stitches, and how many ways there were to do each one. It was boring and tiring, but hey, it's not terribly boring, because despite my best attempts, Meredith was still screeching in my ear.

I pulled out a coffee-flavored doughnut and began to consume it. "I believe that I have had over twenty treats in the past three days. It has been great," I told Meredith absentmindedly.

"Autumn?"

Sapphire!

She was there, with two female beings, a young woman that looked just slightly older than Sapphire and me, and a little girl with a damp dirty face (though we both had dirty faces, mine dirty with doughnut icing, and powdered sugar, and hers with dirt). She looked younger than me, and surely younger than Sapphire. Her build was short and gangly, and she had a rather pleasant expression on her face, despite the other characteristics playing a role on her face.

"How, did you, we were separated—what?!" Sapphire stammered.

"We must have gotten linked back together!" I told her, excited.

"Yes probably," she agreed, sounding more like the cool nonchalant warrior I knew.

"Um, explain." Kris crossed her arms and raised her eyebrows, and Olive looked at Sapphire expectantly.

"Ah, yes, Autumn, this is Kris, Kris this Is Autumn. Olive this is my friend Autumn, Autumn, this is Olive. She was in the prison camp with me when the witches caught us. Oh, and this is Sir, our ride. And this little cutie is Jemima." She took a breath.

"Hey," I greeted all of Sapphire's new-found friends.

"By the way, I adore your hair," Me and Kris complimented at the same time. We both laughed, again at the same time.

"What the heck," Sapphire and Olive rolled their eyes.

We all happily walked, getting to know each other.

Then, I spoke up; "Sapphire, do you remember the witch I told you about? The one that is going to tell you how to fix your fate?"

"Yes, I do, do you know where she is?" Sapphire enquired.

"I don't know, but I do know where witches tend to like to put their homes."

"Then you can go ahead and lead me to where you think one is."

"Ok," I answered, and began to look for the terrain witches found most comfortable: swampy areas, deep in the forest, guarded by layers of trees.

I heard Kris ask Sapphire a few questions, Sapphire answered, and then Kris nodded.

We walked on until we hit a small cottage. *BINGO!* I thought with deep satisfaction. Here was our target.

A new problem was presented to us. How were we to get in? We couldn't just walk right in unannounced.

But before anything could happen, Sapphire and Kris walked right in front of me and rapped on the door.

Chapter Eight

Basically an HOUR after I had rapped on the solid wooden door, it opened. Behind it, was a black cat, then a couple milliseconds later, a middle-aged woman appeared from behind the open door. The cat quickly ran up her black dress, and settled herself on the woman's shoulder.

"Did I fool you?"

I rolled my eyes in rage as she realized that I had wondered if there was anyone in the cottage.

"Yes I see." The woman's eyes were gleaming now. "Please, come. I am a seer, and yes I do know that you are looking for me and need answers, so come please!" The witch narrowed her eyes in both preparation and annoyance.

The room was warm, and smelled like cats and coffee. I immediately knew that this woman was obsessed with cats.

"She is–" Kris blurted unexpectedly. And then gave a nervous laugh.

"What, I asked her," not knowing if I had heard right.

"She's a mind reader." The witch plopped down on the chair announcing Kris's secret to the world.

"Is it true?" I asked Kris.

She quietly nodded her head.

"That explains a lot," was all I could manage.

Kris looked at her feet.

"I'm sorry for not telling you, I—"

"Kris you're fine." I went over and hugged her. She was perfect just the way she was.

"Ok." Kris twisted her head.

"Well, now that we got a superb start to our conversation, let's talk about Sapphire and her fate, and choices." She blinked at me, wearing the most fake 'innocent' smile the universe had laid eyes on.

I could have pinched her.

Nevertheless, I began to tell her about my story.

* * * * *

"So you came across tulips didn't you?" the witch asked with that awful gleam in her eye.

"Well yes, I did. As I told you, it turned the purple that means you screwed up, and now I don't know what to do, or what I did wrong, and I was wondering if you could look into the past and tell me what I did wrong," I gushed.

"Here's the thing, witches are no more powerful than your friend Kris here. We are sometimes telepaths, or seers, but that is the only 'superpower' that we possess. We are simply book-drag-ons, who appreciate knowledge, and desire to share it. Now here is the knowledge that I have. The tulips are bossy little creatures that want to control you. DO NOT think that they know your past, or anything about you. The truth is that they just think you're 'mean.' It is their opinion. Maybe they have noticed you hunting in their part of the forest, and think you are doing it for fun, and don't know that you need to do it for your survival.

"The question you need to ask yourself is if it is bad. So with that spoken you pretty much have your answer." She sipped her tea and beamed at me.

I was furious.

I had just wasted an ENTIRE WEEK OF MY LIFE FRETTING OVER FLOWERS, AND STUPID FATE.

"May I just say that we have cats, and they are willing to cuddle so, yeah." Autumn briskly nodded to Kris to get Jemima for me to play with while I calmed my enraged nerves.

And then we hopped on Sir, and flew home.

Chapter Nine

I approached my small cottage, Kris had kindly dropped all of us off at our separate locations.

It had all been decided that Olive was to live with Autumn. Autumn would make Olive happy, and Olive would contain Autumn, and keep her from going mad. I figured it would be fine, I would just check on them once in a while.

I opened the door to my home and there was Ruelian. I told her I was home, and after a reprimand and a hug, I went upstairs to think.

* * * * *

I had gathered my thoughts. I had new friends, and I had met tons of new people (and animals). It was a beautiful adventure that I had taken myself on.

Maggie Frazer: artist, scientist, author, sister, granddaughter, niece, and teller of stories.

{thanks to a beautiful, and loving audience.}